The edge of forever

Pearls of Noor

To those who have been met at the edge,

And to those who are still waiting.

Perhaps the deepest form of love

is the love that we give

when we awaken half an hour

before Fajr salah

and whisper the words of our love

before our Lord

- Tahajjud

I craved him

like he was a part of my heart

that had been separated from my soul

And the sound of his name

was more familiar to me

than the sound of my own beating heart.

I would still find a thousand ways

to tell you I love you

even if my mouth was sewn shut

even if my body could not move

In the depth of the night

before your face had ever met mine

my soul met yours

hiding somewhere

in the secret parts of my heart

as I whispered a name in prayer

that I did not yet know

'And after everything,

why do you still choose me?'

'Because I love you

as much as I love to breathe.'

They warned me about your fire

and whispered about its destruction

telling me that everything it touched

went up in flames

So I jumped in

just to feel your warmth

A mere exhale from you

in my direction

fills my heart with air

until it swells in my chest

Yet the sharpness of your absence

becomes the prick of a thorn

belonging to a rose I once loved

How can I forget you

when your name

is inscribed upon my breath?

You entered my heart without knocking

and stayed as if it were your own home

In a room full of a thousand lovers

I'd leave

and look for you

And when your heart is still aching

deep into the night

just know that the pain is from Allah

and also from Allah

is the relief that will follow.

'With hardship comes ease.'

I am unsure

whether it would cause me more pain

to forget you

or remember you for the rest of my life

For your memory washes over me

every now and again

like the tide

and each time

a part of me crumbles away

like sea foam

Each time I think of you

my heart swells with indignation

in my chest

for the only way you allow me

to adore you

is through words

that you will never even read

His hair was so black

it reminded me of the night sky

and when he smiled there'd be light

that's why I called him the moon

You have no clue

that the whole sun burns just for you

One day you will find someone worthy

of the love you have to give

and they will return it to you

Tenfold

And even if the distance between us

remains that of one thousand oceans

I'll wait for you patiently

with the certainty of the sea

before it is reunited with its shore

Until then I will love you

from the distance at which

the sky loves the sea

hoping my duas find their way

to your lonely heart

Every time I saw you smile

I became convinced that

sadness was a lie

We spoke in gestures more than words

like you cooking my favourite food

each time I visited your home

and every flower in the supermarket

calling your name

the rattle of your bangles

and the silky soft touch of your saris

and constantly hearing a chorus of

'eat more'

was enough to understand

what it meant to build a home

despite our estranged tongues and

foreign words

the care still seeped

between the sentences

and the smile spreading to the creases

under both of your eyes

with each line being traced back

to what it meant to love

    - for my Nanu

I'd hand you my heart in seconds

because it is yours

before it has ever been mine

and I think of you

in the space between each beat

The first time I heard your laugh

was the first time I arrived home

To me

your voice is medicine

and I whisper your name

like it's a vow

When our eyes met for the first time

I just knew that our hearts

had done this before

If I threw every thought I had about you

into the ocean

the sea would speak about your eyes

every time the sun sparkled down on it

and each time the waves

crashed onto the shore

it would sound like your voice

It's hard to know when exactly

you've fallen in love with someone.

It creeps up on you

and suddenly you just *are,*

 before you even know it's happened.

I think you know you love someone

when you'd do anything for them

and a part of what makes you

you

is the part that loves them

And where if you take that love away

there is nothing left

- Part 1 of the conversations we never had

My heart

asked my Lord for you the other day

did you feel it?

As long as I am alive

and you are with me

I am more of myself

when I am loving you

than when I am called my own name

If his name is written beside yours

not even all the oceans' waters

could wash away the ink

What is supposed to reach you

will always

find you.

You rise every morning

and fall to slumber in the night

not knowing that you live both

on this earth

and in my mind

You remain so unaware

that every word I write that hits paper

is born only after my pen

whispers your name

Your name is etched into my duas

and I think of you so often

that sometimes I am more you

than myself

You have made a home out of my prayers.

I pray for you to love Allah

and to be loved by Allah

I pray for your peace,

your success,

your comfort

I pray to become your peace

watch your success

and to bring you comfort

I pray to be your shelter from the cold

and your rock

when the earth around you shakes

And I pray

to soon

learn your name

'Do you love me?

'No.'

'No?'

'Not yet, but I think one day I will…

…You're literally everything

I've been looking for

handed to me on a silver platter.'

- Part 2 of the conversations we never had

I do not know what is harder

to lose you

or to leave you

You are the captivating wonder

and beautiful contradiction

that comes with seeing the moon in

daylight

for the very first time

And perhaps you are only beautiful

because you are just like the moon

bright, shining

and so far away

With each second that passes by

you are a moment closer

to being reunited with your Loved One

once again in this life

to mark the start of your

Forever

Do not wish your present away whilst dreaming about your future, for your parents are growing old, and your brother won't be this little forever.

One day you'll yearn to go back to the life you live right now.

If I could measure my love for you

every scale on the planet would break

I don't know what there exists more of

stars in the sky

or times I've mentioned your name

in my duas

I could fill libraries worth of books

just describing why I love

a single strand of hair on your head

And if I ever saw you in pain

my tears would be so abundant

that even the oceans

would feel thirsty

They asked me if I could imagine

a life without you

so I asked the forest what it would be

without its trees

and tried to imagine the difference

between a house and home

And the lovers,

they find comfort

in being able to spend Forever

with each other

but with you

even Forever is not long enough

I conquered my mind

to forget the sound of his voice

and I no longer see his smile

every time I close my eyes,

but Ya Rabb, tell me,

why does my heart whisper to You

in sujood

hoping that it echoes the same words

that the pen wrote 50,000 years ago

when precious ink placed

our names beside each other

for the rest of eternity

You say I don't understand silence

but I would rather speak

than die

carrying the weight of one thousand words

upon my crumbling back

After you left

each atom in my body

became infused with memories of you

that it pains my own brain to remember

the way my arms ache

when they cannot hold you

and my legs grow heavy with each step

that does not lead to you

and my heart,

do not ask me about

my bleeding heart

They say you fall in love

with a person's eyes first

because they contain the soul

so I told myself I'd have to sift through the

eyes

of a thousand strangers

only dreaming of one day

looking into yours

never expecting it to be you

but hoping it was anyway

And you will be content

with whatever your Lord

has written for you

not because it's what you want

but because it's what He wants

You let me go for my own good

but did you know

I'd wait for you at the edge of forever?

And when Allah (SWT)

placed Adam (AS) on the earth

he walked across the whole world

in search of his Hawa (AS).

So be still, my sister

your husband will find you

for you are his missing rib

and the other half of his religion

He will come to you

and give you his whole heart

Meeting you felt like

the first sip of coffee

after a lifetime of no sleep

When he realised he loved her,

he thanked his Lord,

because he finally understood

what his heart was made for

And when he held her for the first time

he thanked his Lord again,

because he finally understood

what his arms were made for

The moon is upset with me

and the sky refuses to speak

I don't understand what I have done

or where our love went

And what is worse?

A raging thunder or a silent storm

And my eyes become blind

when faced with your flaws

just how your heart closes

when faced with my love

I ask myself

why can't I see the bad in you

whilst you could never see the good

in me?

All of the good you saw in him

was only there because it existed first

within yourself

How painful it is

to love a mere mirage

and spend life grasping at a shadow

of what never even was

whilst waiting for the end of a story

that was never even written

One day

you will have your morning coffee

with the love of your life

he will look into your sleepy eyes

and see his Forever

and then wonder what life even was

before he met you

Ya Rabb,

Heal whatever it is that is inside my heart

for there is so much of him in it

that I can't tell where he ends

and where my heart begins

You're still in my heart

and my Duas feel incomplete

when they aren't filled with your name

still destiny works against us

for God wrote something else

They left when they saw darkness in you

whilst I ran

towards the beauty of the night

You read millions of love stories

and wonder why you never have your own

but don't forget that your story is written

by the Greatest of all writers

who wrote down every beautiful thing

to have happened in existence,

So bow your head in sujood

and ask for a love greater

than any you've read about

Instead of growing impatient

not knowing that

 if you hadn't closed the book

your love story would be written

on the very next page

And to think

that I've written pages upon pages

of love poetry all about you

before even learning your name

Your soul speaks to me

in ways that words wish they could

for its depth is that

of a thousand oceans

and its beauty striking

like the pale moon

on a summer night's sky

I bow my head in sujood

and as my head touches the ground

I feel my heart swell

as my soul sighs gently

breaths of relief as it speaks to my Lord

and I imagine what it would be like

to bite into the fruit of fresh pomegranate

in *Jannatul Firdaus*

with its heavenly juice

running down my glistening arms

as *Zanjabeel, Kafoor and Tasneem*

whisper my name

in each trickle of water that flows down

my worldly fears having faded away

as I sigh again

this time with breaths of musk

and watch them melt

into the streams of honey

Different forms of love:

When your happiness and theirs are one

The first time he puts a necklace on you

Jewellery passed down from your grandmother

Having your mothers eyes

'I thought of you'

Cooking for others

Giving them what you wish for yourself

Dua

I stood under the pale moonlight last night

as it cast rivers of white

and streams of pearls

cascading down from the

gaps in between the clouds

veiling it gently

like a silken curtain

I thought of my daughter

and how she will have bright eyes

like the moon

with a soul richer

and more beautiful

than the entire night sky

and she will be all of me

And none of you.

She runs wild with the waves

the sea breeze carrying her love

for adventure through her veins

the rock of the family,

her heart full and steady

as it pumps out love

to different homes

there is more love

within her very being

than there exists between most spouses

She has my grandmother's heart

but my grandfather's soul

with her eyes holding the depth of

one thousand oceans

whilst wildfires burn within her

and mountains crumble under her gaze

A woman of contradictions,

so soft yet so strong

with no children of her own

yet full of the love

that can only be felt from a Mother

    - my third Aunt

I ask Al-Wadud to grant us a love
more poignant than the words spoken
within the language of my heart
A love that goes beyond flowers,
anniversaries, and shared secrets

The kind of love that echoes
through history
like the love between the
Prophet (SAW) and Aisha (RA)
where you place your lips
where mine once were on a glass
so that they may meet again
without us even touching

The kind of love

that made one of the strongest men

in the world

Ali (RA)

unable to carry his grief

as he lost his beloved

Fatima (RA)

Prayers where I mention your name

feel like little love letters to Al-Wadud

I first thank Him

for being loved by you

then I beg Him

to increase His love for you

'I don't love you

because of what you've done for me

I love you because of who you are.

Your akhlaq,

the way you carry yourself,

your goals, your hopes, and your dreams,

your kindness,

your humour,

your eyes,

your soul

It's everything about you,

I just love everything.'

- Part 3 of the conversations we never had

And if it is from Love

that I am slowly dying

then you are both the disease

and the cure

She had full cheeks

they were pink and made her look so alive

that if Death itself saw them,

it would leave and come back as Life

He had white pearly teeth

she'd always joke

that they shined like the stars

but what she loved about him most

was his smile

he had the kind of smile

that made even strangers

want to tell him

their deepest darkest secrets

And when they could touch

for the first time

he held her like he was suffocating

and she was oxygen itself

All it took

was just one pair of eyes

and a smile that met them

like they were old friends

and I knew I'd be happy

never seeing anything else

for the rest of my life

Understand your value

run to the One who sees your worth

for He is the One who created it

run back to Allah

who awaits you with open arms

And now when it rains

I only thank my Lord

ever since my Duas for you

became my umbrella

He sends me His mercy

and I send Him my love for you

Her beauty is the first thing you notice

when you meet her

but it's the last thing that comes to mind

when you think of all the reasons

for why you love her

Sometimes when Allah tests your patience

it's not a test of how patient you'll be

until He grants you what you want.

Sometimes it's a test

of how patient you'll be

when He does not.

Sometimes Allah will place a desire

so strong in your heart

that it burns

and you'll call out to Him in

desperation

before realising that the test

you called Desire

was a measure of your patience

and that if Allah doesn't give you

your wish

your reward will be so much better.

Would we now be beside each other had we met any sooner?

If you searched my Duas,

not once

would you find your own name

for my love for you

goes beyond words

and belongs to the

Duas of the Heart

Ya Sami,

When he calls out to you

hear his prayers

even the ones

that his heart makes in secret

I took the pain that you gave me

and awoke

ten minutes before fajr

then I turned it

into 12 love letters to Allah.

For in each sujood

of each rakat

I mentioned your name

and begged Him

to heal

and mend

the wounds you left inside my chest

For my happiness

I think of your eyes

and the way they hold the universe

As for my sorrows,

I have my mat

and a thousand conversations with Allah

Sometimes I tell the wind

about your voice

and think even the stars

are jealous of your eyes.

By now,

even the moon

must know your name.

The first time I learnt your name

I thought I heard

'Forever.'

But the last time I looked into your eyes,

it was as if someone had told me

'This is the last time you'll ever drink tea.'

Ya roohi, ya roohi, ya roohi

I whispered to you

as you lay fast asleep

your gentle breaths dissolving

into the breeze of a summer night

Ya albi, ya albi, ya albi

The day we met

I felt like a piece of my heart

had been replaced by you

Ya hayati, ya hayati, ya hayati

When our fingers touched for the first time

you were as familiar to me

as the blood running through my veins

so then you became

my lifeline

The peeling of pomegranates

is a love language

that is passed down from

mother to daughter

for more generations going back in time

than there are seeds

in the ruby red fruit

bloodlines running deeper

and richer

than the juices

running down my mother's hands

They say

'when you know you know'

For it is the moment you meet

the one whose Rib

became your entire being

in the sense that the whole of you

is a part of him

incomplete

until reunited with your very existence

A soul tie

that was written with his name

next to yours

way before the sky ever met the sea

with every atom in creation

making up the story

that leads to the moment

where the Rib finds the Body

it belongs to

and the Soul finds its companion

This is how before you even know

You'll Know.

And I pray that the one that comes after

loves you harder

loves you better

and that his words heal

the secret cries you suppress

at the end of each breath

and his touch softens

the hardening of your heart,

I pray that he loves you

like the poetry you read

and that each mundane moment with him

makes life feel like the dreams

you never thought could come true

I pray that he becomes a

walking living breathing

slice of Jannah

on this earth

here to remind you of

Allah's love and mercy

as He bestowed upon you the Final relief

whose arrival you waited for

when the test was at its hardest

I hear your breaths in the wind

and the sound of your voice

even within silence

you are long gone

but I cannot let go

How do I forget you?

I walked away from you

but still your ghost walks beside me

and torments me with your smile

and the only time

I ever looked into your eyes

I still search for you

in every lover

how do I forget your voice?

Why can't you leave me

even long after you have gone?

As I knelt down to make sujood

the barriers guarding my emotions

melted away

for even the strongest of steel

cannot withstand the warmth

I feel when I speak with my Lord

you don't have to be so strong all the time

I tell myself

before I cry to Al-Waliy,

the Protective Friend who honoured me

with the pain I carry

and who gave me the relief

of letting it slide down my back

five times a day

five times a day

I let my guard down

and I just crumble

in front of my Lord

when even I am sick

of my own thoughts

so I turn them off

and let Him hear my silent duas

for there are few things

as beloved

as the stories the heart tells

to its Maker

My mother has never told me

that she loves me

but I remember hearing stories

of how ill and weak she was

before I was born

how the start of my life

could have been the end of hers

and that I cried all night

whilst during the days she took care of me

before taking care of herself

I recently asked her

'did you ever wish you could go back

for a day after I was born?'

I wanted to know if she ever wanted

her old life back

in those moments where it got tough

just for a day

she was shocked by my question

and shook her head

she told me that her only regret

was not having me sooner

so that we could have had more time

despite the pain

the cries

the sleepless nights and suffering

she would have embraced

more of these moments

just to be around me for even longer

so every day I pray to have

Forever with her

in Allah's Jannah

which just so obviously

lies beneath her very feet

I can't tell if the burning inside my chest

after you left

is my heart racing

to catch up with my head

or if it is yearning to tell me something

that my head does not yet know

- *be patient with your heart*

- *let it catch up*

Who loves me more?

I ask myself

my head or my heart?

My head

who leads me

and tries to protect me

from the whimsical ways of the heart

or my heart

who casts away logic

and basks me in made-up love

I always had a soft spot

for my heart

for my head taunts it

and deems it weak

fragile

vulnerable

naive

for believing that fairy tales

could ever come true

but little does my head know,

the heart possesses a single type of power

to embrace emotion

rather than hide

to surrender and give into its reign

instead of temporarily casting it aside

like the cowardly brain

afraid to be seen or heard

trembling behind the mirage

of nonchalance

secretly hoping that the heart would win

for the clean ones always do, in the end

One day I'll tell my daughter about you

when her heart breaks for the first time

and I'll call you my Parallel Lover

I'll tell her about the way we aligned

and how our morals

virtues,

hopes and dreams

were all laid out in front of us

pointing in the same direction

and we walked towards them together

but also each as one

gazing in each other's direction

with our eyes

never quite being able to meet

clouded by the distance between us

labelled

'right person, wrong time'

Your heart to my soul

is what the moon is

to the sky

all of nature echoes

the story of you and I

If I looked back

I'd say it was nothing

even though it felt like

everything at the time,

it wasn't anything really,

because our paths only crossed once,

and he probably doesn't remember

much about me at all

but I won't forget the fact that

he has his coffee with two sugars

because his mum does too,

or how shocked I was

when he ordered it with oat milk,

I'll always remember his favourite food,

film

and football team,

the story of how his sister met her husband

and the way he'd tell me 'acha'

instead of 'okay'

I didn't even know his favourite colour

but I knew that he smiled

more than he laughed

in fact he didn't used to laugh very often

so I always felt special

each time a deep chuckle

would escape from his lips

after I made some dumb joke.

I liked the way he turned into a little kid

when he smiled

and how it always met his eyes

'ocean eyes' they reminded me of

even though they were brown

but they were just so warm

and held so much depth.

He claimed to have awful dress sense,

but I thought

he had the best taste in the world.

He was cultured

smart

intelligent

interesting

but he hid behind the person

he'd always wanted to be

so I felt like I never really knew him

We had the time

but we just kept missing each other

it wasn't meant to be

but it could've been.

My memories of him are so blurry,

half of them probably made up

by my own head,

but my feelings as sharp

as the coldness he sometimes carried,

which always took me by surprise.

Probably because I never actually

knew him

even though I could've done

and were there any good in the situation,

I think I really would've done.

Acknowledgements

Thank you to my family,

whose support shined through

to illuminate dreams

they didn't even know I had.

Thank you to my friends,

who with open arms

share the burden

of carrying my heart

when it gets too heavy.

To my readers,

for their support and

to the small pieces of my soul.

And lastly,

thank you to Allah,

the Most Gracious, the Most Merciful,

the One who makes it all possible.

Printed in Great Britain
by Amazon